Dear Parent:
Your child's love of reading starts here!

Every child learns to read in a different way and at his or her own speed. Some go back and forth between reading levels and read favorite books again and again. Others read through each level in order. You can help your young reader improve and become more confident by encouraging his or her own interests and abilities. From books your child reads with you to the first books he or she reads alone, there are I Can Read Books for every stage of reading:

SHARED READING
Basic language, word repetition, and whimsical illustrations, ideal for sharing with your emergent reader

BEGINNING READING
Short sentences, familiar words, and simple concepts for children eager to read on their own

READING WITH HELP
Engaging stories, longer sentences, and language play for developing readers

READING ALONE
Complex plots, challenging vocabulary, and high-interest topics for the independent reader

ADVANCED READING
Short paragraphs, chapters, and exciting themes for the perfect bridge to chapter books

I Can Read Books have introduced children to the joy of reading since 1957. Featuring award-winning authors and illustrators and a fabulous cast of beloved characters, I Can Read Books set the standard for beginning readers.

A lifetime of discovery begins with the magical words **"I Can Read!"**

Visit www.icanread.com for information
on enriching your child's reading experience.

To Peter and Laura
with love
—A.S.C.

For all the dedicated
Cat Rescue volunteers
—P.M.

I Can Read Book® is a trademark of HarperCollins Publishers.

Scat, Cat! Text copyright © 2010 by Alyssa Satin Capucilli Illustrations copyright © 2010 by Paul Meisel All rights reserved. Printed in the United States of America. No part of this book may be used or reproduced in any manner whatsoever without written permission except in the case of brief quotations embodied in critical articles and reviews. For information address HarperCollins Children's Books, a division of HarperCollins Publishers, 10 East 53rd Street, New York, NY 10022. www.icanread.com

Library of Congress Cataloging-in-Publication Data is available.
ISBN 978-0-06-117754-5 (trade bdg.) — ISBN 978-0-06-117756-9 (pbk.)

10 11 12 13   LP/WOR 10 9 8 7 6 5 4 3 2 ❖   First Edition

Scat, Cat!

story by Alyssa Satin Capucilli

pictures by Paul Meisel

HARPER

An Imprint of HarperCollinsPublishers

There was a cat.

It was a small cat.

It was a striped cat.

It was a lost cat.

The cat walked and walked.

"Scat, cat!" said the dog.

"Scat, cat!" said the bird.

"Scat, cat!" said the other cats.

"Go home."

So the cat walked and walked some more.

"Scat, cat!" said the barber.

"Scat, cat!" said the baker.

"Scat, cat!" said the bus driver.

"Go home."

The cat kept walking.

"Scat, cat!" said the duck.

"Scat, cat!" said the frog.

"Scat, cat!" said the goose.

"Go home."

The cat walked and walked
until the sky grew dark.
"Scat, cat!" said the owl.

"Scat, cat!" said the bat.

The cat curled up in a log.
"That's my log!"
said the skunk. "Scat, cat!"

So the cat walked and walked.
And the cat walked and walked
some more.

The cat walked until he came
to a little house.

The tired cat climbed the steps
and curled up on a soft pillow.

And there, the small cat
fell fast asleep
under the starry sky.

When morning came,
the cat stretched.

The cat yawned.

The cat blinked its eyes.

There was a little boy.

The little boy did not say,
"Scat, cat!"

He said,

"Where have you been, cat?

I have been looking for you

everywhere!"

"Mew, mew, mew!"
said the small cat.

It was good to be home.